DEAR MOUSE FRIENDS, WELCOME TO THE

STONE AGE!

Welcome to the Stone Age . . . and the world of the cavemice!

Capital: Old Mouse City

Population: We're not sure. (Math doesn't exist yet!) But besides cavemice, there are plenty of dinosaurs, <u>way</u> too many saber-toothed tigers, and ferocious cave bears — but no mouse has ever had the courage to count them!

Typical Food: Petrified cheese soup

National Holiday: **Great Zap Day**, which celebrates the discovery of fire. Rodents exchange grilled cheese sandwiches on this holiday.

National Drink: Mammoth milkshakes

Climate: Unpredictable, with frequent meteor showers

cheese soup

milkshake

Money

Seashells of all shapes and sizes

Measurement

The basic unit of measurement is based on the length of the tail of the leader of the village. A unit can be divided into a half tail or quarter tail. The leader is always ready to present his tail when there is a dispute.

THE CAVEMICE

Geronimo

Trap

Thea

Benjamin

Bugsy Wugsy

Hercule Poirat

Grandma Ratrock

Geronimo Stilton

CAVEMICE

SHOO, CAVEFLIES!

Scholastic Inc.

Copyright © 2014 by Edizioni Piemme S.p.A., Palazzo Mondadori, Via Mondadori 1, 20090 Segrate, Italy. International Rights © Atlantyca S.p.A. English translation © 2017 by Atlantyca S.p.A.

The publisher does not have any control over and does not assume any responsibility for author or third-party websites or their content.

GERONIMO STILTON names, characters, and related indicia are copyright, trademark, and exclusive license of Atlantyca S.p.A. All rights reserved. The moral right of the author has been asserted. Based on an original idea by Elisabetta Dami. www.geronimostilton.com

Published by Scholastic Inc., *Publishers since 1920*, 557 Broadway, New York, NY 10012. SCHOLASTIC and associated logos are trademarks and/or registered trademarks of Scholastic Inc.

Stilton is the name of a famous English cheese. It is a registered trademark of the Stilton Cheese Makers' Association. For more information, go to www.stiltoncheese.com.

This book is a work of fiction. Names, characters, places, and incidents are either the product of the author's imagination or are used fictitiously, and any resemblance to actual persons, living or dead, business establishments, events, or locales is entirely coincidental.

ISBN 978-1-338-08866-3

Text by Geronimo Stilton
Original title *Non svegliate le mosche ronf ronf!*
Cover by Flavio Ferron
Illustrations by Giuseppe Facciotto (pencils), Carolina Livio (inks), and Daniele Verzini and Valeria Cairoli (color)
Graphics by Marta Lorini

Special thanks to Kathryn Cristaldi
Translated by Julia Heim
Interior design by Becky James

10 9 8 7 6 5 4 3 2 1   17 18 19 20 21

Printed in the U.S.A.   40
First printing 2017

MANY AGES AGO, ON PREHISTORIC MOUSE ISLAND, THERE WAS A VILLAGE CALLED OLD MOUSE CITY. IT WAS INHABITED BY BRAVE *RODENT SAPIENS* KNOWN AS THE CAVEMICE. DANGERS SURROUNDED THE MICE AT EVERY TURN: EARTHQUAKES, METEOR SHOWERS, FEROCIOUS DINOSAURS, AND FIERCE GANGS OF SABER-TOOTHED TIGERS. BUT THE BRAVE CAVEMICE FACED IT ALL WITH A SENSE OF HUMOR, AND WERE ALWAYS READY TO LEND A HAND TO OTHERS.

HOW DO I KNOW THIS? I DISCOVERED AN ANCIENT BOOK WRITTEN BY MY ANCESTOR, GERONIMO STILTONOOT! HE CARVED HIS STORIES INTO STONE TABLETS AND ILLUSTRATED THEM WITH HIS ETCHINGS.

I AM PROUD TO SHARE THESE STONE AGE STORIES WITH YOU. THE EXCITING ADVENTURES OF THE CAVEMICE WILL MAKE YOUR FUR STAND ON END, AND THE JOKES WILL TICKLE YOUR WHISKERS! HAPPY READING!

Geronimo Stilton

WARNING! DON'T IMITATE THE CAVEMICE. WE'RE NOT IN THE STONE AGE ANYMORE!

PICKAX HAS RETURNED!

It was a mouserific spring morning. The cactus flowers were **blooming**, the pterodactyls were **cawing**, and a cool breeze was **blowing**. What a perfect day for a celebration in *Old Mouse City*!

On that day, the greatest explorer in prehistory, **PALEO PICKAX**, was returning from his latest exploration. Oh, I'm so scatterbrained — I haven't introduced myself yet! My name is Stiltonoot, **GERONIMO STILTONOOT**, and I am the publisher of *The Stone Gazette*, the most famouse newspaper in prehistory (*umm* . . . it's also the only one)!

PALEO PICKAX is one of the many friends I've met during my cavemouse adventures. I don't know if you know this, but a few months ago Pickax set off for a place called **Mount Mishmash**, and hc's been living there ever since! No one has ever been there before (well, except Pickax!), and legend has it, the weather there is very **STRANGE**. In one small area, you can find mountains, the desert, snow, the forest, a **volcano**, and even a **river** full of fish!

Anyway, as I was saying, that

PALEO PICKAX
IN ACTION

It's really him. It's Pickax!

morning at dawn, **LEO EDISTONE**, the village inventor, pointed the longeye, our prehistoric telescope, toward the horizon.

"It's Paleo Pickax!" Leo gasped.

Immediately, Gossip Radio, the most confusing radio station in prehistory (run by my rival, **SALLY ROCKMOUSEN**), spread the word.

"**SPECIAL EDITIOOOONN!**," the first shouter from Gossip Radio yelled. "Pickax has returned!"

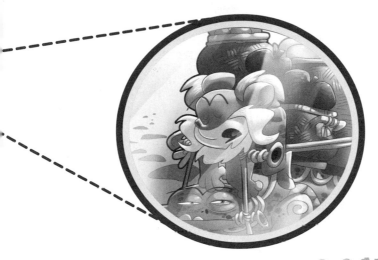

"SPECIAL EDITIOOOONN!" the second shouter called. "Pickax has been burned!"

"SPECIAL EDITIOOOONN!" the third shouter yelled. "Sick rats have been burned and churned into cheese!"

HOLEY BOULDERS, WHAT RIDICULOUS JOURNALISTS!

To spread the news the right way, Old Mouse City needed a **REAL** journalist (which I am proud to report I am!). So, still **half asleep**, I darted to the wall that surrounds our city. Almost all my fellow citizens were gathered there, including my candid sister, Thea, and my **obnoxious** cousin Trap.

"Well, look who made it out of his cave before **noon** today!" my cousin teased. "Thanks for joining us."

"Of course I'm here," I squeaked, **ROLLING** my eyes. "I'm the only one who can **report** the news responsibly."

Meanwhile, the citizens of Old Mouse City waited impatiently for Pickax to appear.

"What do you think Pickax brought back for his **beloved** village leader?" Ernest Heftymouse wondered aloud.

"Maybe he found a pretty dress for me," his daughter, Harriet Heftymouse, added. "But then, everything looks pretty on me, right, Geronimo?"

I gulped.

Harriet had a huge **crush** on me. Though I didn't feel the same way, I didn't want to be rude.

"Y-yes," I stammered. "Uh, very p-pretty."

By then Pickax was at the doors of Old Mouse City.

He was sitting on the back of a CARTOSAURUS with a caravan of other cartosauruses bearing gifts following close behind. The explorer wore a WHITE beard, a happy smile, and . . .

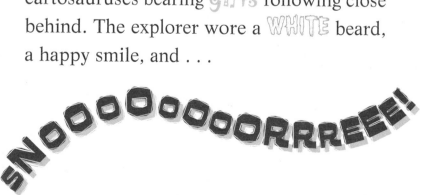

SNOOOOOOOORRREEE!

7

Suddenly, Pickax was struck by one of his famouse STONE AGE SLUMBERS!

That's right — our explorer friend is also known throughout the land for one strange trait: He falls asleep without warning! And nothing — not even the trumpeting from the horn of a TRICERATOPS — can wake him!

At that exact moment, **disaster** struck.

"Look!" Thea shrieked.

You're trapped!

We turned to find **TIGER KHAN**, the fanged leader of the terrible saber-toothed tigers, and his band of felines **DROOLING** over Pickax!

NOT US!

Ernest Heftymouse encouraged the citizens of Old Mouse City to HELP their fellow rodent.

"**COME ON, EVERYONE!**" he squeaked. "Pickax is about to be **devoured** by the saber-toothed tigers! We've got to save him! Who's with me?!"

No one squeaked. I noticed Timidtail was trying to sneak off to his cave, and Worrywhiskers had just fainted.

Fossilized feta! Things were not looking good. Pickax was a courageous mouse. In fact, he was incredibly **TOUGH**. But how tough can a cavemouse possibly be

when he's sound asleep?!

Luckily, my sister, Thea, took control. **"I'll handle this!"** she insisted, facing the crowd. "Citizens of Old Mouse City, who hates the great explorer **PICKAX**?" she asked.

The cavemice looked confused.

Um...Er... Uh...

"Um, not us," they murmured.

"Well, who likes **TIGER KHAN** and his band of cats?"

This time, the cavemice responded louder.

"Not us!" they chorused.

"And who would like those rotten cats to eat all the delicious treats Pickax

brought to share with his fellow cavemice?"

At this, my fellow cave rodents jumped up.

"**Not us!**" they shrieked.

"Then let's go get them!" Thea cried.

And so the citizens of Old Mouse City scampered to Pickax's rescue, shouting out like a gang of yellosauruses.

Meanwhile, the saber-toothed tigers were already **digging** through the food strapped to the backs of the cartosauruses.

"Well, well, what do we have here?" Tiger Khan sneered. "You're so kind to bring us these delicacies. We'll eat them first before we gobble up you dirty rats!"

Right at that moment, Pickax woke up. He spotted Tiger Khan pawing through his gifts and let out a defiant squeak.

"STOP RIGHT THERE!" he shrieked.

Then he grabbed his club and **HIT** the feline leader right on the noggin.

BOOOONNNKKK!

A loud echo followed.

"Of course your big head sounds completely EMPTY," Pickax observed.

Tiger Khan let out a roar.

Take that!

Youch!

But before he snagged Pickax, one of the saber-toothed tigers interrupted.

"Um, **BOSS**, we might need to think of another *meal plan*," he suggested, pointing.

Tiger Khan stopped and looked over his shoulder. Thea had done a fabumouse job rallying the troops. By now, the entire population of *Old Mouse City* was *CHARGING* toward the tigers! Thea was in the lead, swinging *wildly* with her club and sending the giant cats fleeing with their paws up.

Tiger Khan urged his nasty cats to counterattack. But not everyone listened. Some of those cats were afraid!

Still others couldn't refuse their boss.

"Let's turn these **CAVEMICE** into *cavemush*!" Tiger Khan growled, cheering them on.

At that moment, my cousin Trap grabbed a huge bunch of bananas from a cartosaurus. He **launched** the bananas at the pack leader, hitting him in the snout.

SMACK!

A big cloud of flies rose out of the bananas. They swarmed around the leader of the saber-toothed tigers.

Then the strangest thing happened. One of the flies bit **TIGER KHAN** on the shoulder and then **chomped** on my cousin Trap's tail.

Within seconds, the two rivals

collapsed on the ground and began snoring away.

Pickax turned as pale as a slice of fossilized mozzarella.

"Oh no, not them, too," he whispered.

I wanted to ask Pickax what he meant, but there was no time. A SNARLING saber-toothed tiger was headed my way!

BACK-BREAKING BOULDERS! I was done for, finished, **EXTINCT!**

STONE AGE SLUMBER

I closed my eyes, preparing for **premature** extinction, when Thea rushed to my rescue.

"Take that, you oversized kitty!" she squeaked, chucking a **GIANT** watermelon at the **FEROCIOUS** saber-toothed tiger. The fruit **SPLATTERED** all over the place as I raced for safety.

Phew — saved by a whisker!

More caveflies swarmed out of the fruit.

Bzzzzzzzzzzzzzzzzzzzzzzzzzzz!

"Shoo, caveflies!" Thea ordered. Then she grabbed an armful of melons and began **rolling** them at the oncoming saber-toothed tigers.

Ernest Heftymouse and the rest of the cavemice joined in. The tigers did their best to avoid the JUICY obstacles, but soon they were getting hit by more than just a few melons. Heads of crisp lettuce struck them between the shoulders, tomatoes splattered over their fur, and bits of carrots stuck in their whiskers.

What a Jurassic **food fight**!

The tigers were so busy fending off the fruit and vegetables they didn't notice the dinosaurs that were GALLOPING toward them.

BONES AND STONES!

They were the Old Mouse City dinosaurs, and they were led by Thea's autosaurus, Grunty!

It didn't take long for the dinosaurs to trample over the nasty cats.

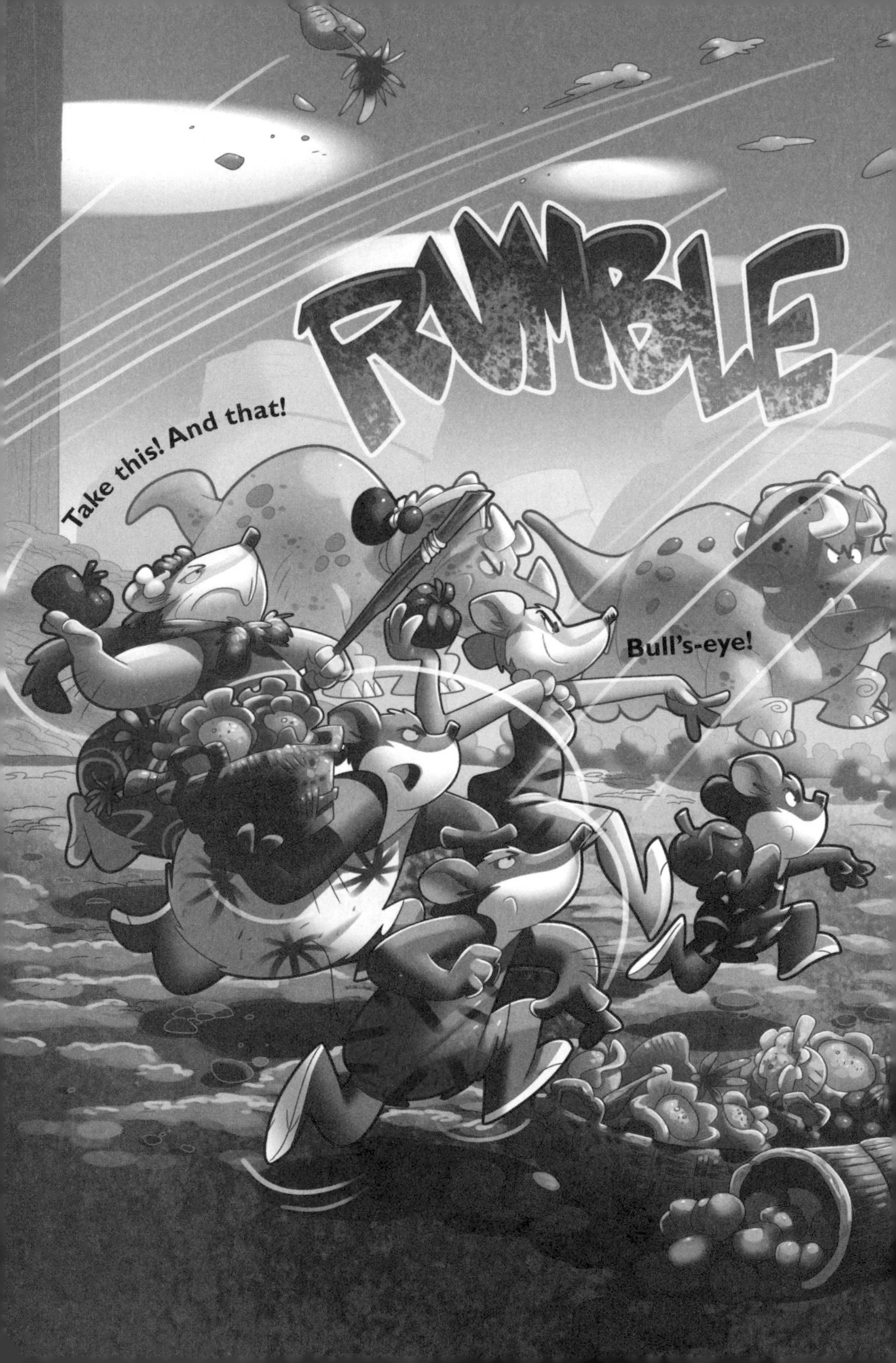
RUMBLE
Take this! And that!
Bull's-eye!

"**Oww!**" yelped a saber-toothed tiger.
"**EVERY CAT FOR HIMSELF!**" meowed
another.

"**WAA! I WANT MY MOMMY!**" wailed a third.

The felines were wiped out like Paleozoic
BOWLING PINS! They **dragged** the sleeping
Tiger Khan with them as they scurried away.
But two **FEROCIOUS FELINES** managed to
hide behind a bush. Unfortunately, none of
us cavemice noticed. We were too excited
celebrating our victory over the rest of
the tigers.

"Yippee!"

"Hooray!"

"We did it!"

Thea wrapped **Grunty** in a warm hug.
"You're my favorite autosaurus in the
PREHISTORIC world!" she squeaked.

Now we only had one **little** problem to

solve. Trap had fallen asleep again and was snoring up a **storm**!

"How is it possible that he can sleep with all this **racket**?!" I wondered aloud.

Right then I heard a sound.

Bzzzᶻzᶻzᶻᶻzᶻzᶻᶻzzᶻzᶻᶻzᶻzᶻz!

The pesky fly that had nipped Trap and Tiger Khan was still *flying* around. Pickax

tried to shoo him away with a palm leaf, but he had no luck.

"What kind of strange fly is this?" Thea asked, curious.

"It's not just any fly," Pickax explained. "It's the terrible snoozer fly! Its sting causes a strange illness — the STONE AGE SLUMBER. It's the same illness that I suffer from!"

"Really?" Thea squeaked, her eyes growing WIDE. "You mean you were stung by that little pest?"

Pickax confirmed that he had been stung many years ago.

"In those days, though, I didn't know there was a remedy," he added.

I was just about to ask about the cure when I saw something move in the bushes. I sniffed the air suspiciously.

SNIFF! SNIFF! SNIFF!!

"**HOLEY BOULDERS**, I smell tiger!" I cried.

"Oh, calm down, scaredy-mouse!" my sister scolded. "The cats are gone! Now, let's hear about that remedy."

Pickax explained that the only way to cure the **STONE AGE SLUMBER** was to drink a tea

Snoozer Flies

WHERE THEY LIVE: WHEREVER THERE'S SOMEONE TO STING

DEFINING TRAIT: MEGALITHIC STINGER

WHAT THEY EAT: THEY LOVE THE HONEY OF JURASSIC BEES

FLIGHT SPEED: THREE TAILS PER HOUR (SLOW AND STEADY WINS THE RACE!)

made from the petals of the **putrid pee-yoo flower**.

"The tea needs to be consumed within THREE DAYS of the bite," Pickax continued.

"Well, what are we waiting for?" Thea responded. "Let's go **FIND** some!"

Unfortunately, finding **putrid pee-yoo flowers** wasn't going to be easy. Pickax explained that the flower was extremely rare.

"I myself have traveled the world up and down and left and right, and I have **never** seen one!" he said.

"**ROCKY RATTRAPS!**" I squeaked. "It sounds hopeless!"

"Not completely," Pickax went on. "I said *I* had never seen one, but there is someone in *Old Mouse City* who has . . ."

"Who?" Thea asked eagerly.

But right then Pickax's eyes closed and . . .

ZZZZZZZZZ!

He fell fast asleep!

"WHO COULD IT BE?" Thea wondered.

Meanwhile, behind the bushes, the hidden saber-toothed tigers were asking themselves the very same question.

Who could it be?

Who could it be?

STICK OUT YOUR TONGUE!

Thea and I loaded Pickax and Trap onto **Grunty** and returned to Old Mouse City.

Just as we arrived, my cousin woke up.

"Hey, what happened?" he asked. "Where are the tigers? Where's **TIGER KHAN**? Let me at him!"

He **punched** the air with his paws.

"Uh, the tigers took off a while ago," I informed him.

Then Thea explained how the **snoozer fly** had stung him. She also told him about the **putrid pee-yoo flower**, the only cure for the **STONE AGE SLUMBER**.

"You mean to tell me that now I'll have the

STONE AGE SLUMBER, too?!" Trap exclaimed.

At first I thought he was upset about the news. But then I noticed a huge smile PLASTERED on Trap's snout.

"This is great!" he announced. "Finally I have the perfect excuse to sleep as much as I like! I can just curl up in my cave and chill like a woolly mammoth!"

My sister and I looked at each other in a panic. Then Thea turned to my cousin.

"Of course, you could sleep as much as you want, Trap," she began, "but imagine this: You're about to bite into a delicious piece of cheesy toast and — **BAM**! You start snoring!"

Trap turned pale.

"Or you fix yourself a nice SUN-MELTED cheddar soup," Thea continued, "and — **BOOM**! You fall dead asleep with your face in your clay bowl!"

Trap's eyes opened **WIDE** in horror.

"**HOLEY MEGALOSAURUS**, what a **NIGHTMARE**!" he exclaimed. "Sun-melted cheddar soup is my favorite!"

Then he began to wail uncontrollably, like a little cavemouselet. He loudly **blew** his nose on my outfit. **Honk!**

"Cousin, please save me from this tragedy!" he cried. "Find me that flower! Get me the cure! Please, you've got to **HELP ME**!"

HONK?!

Save me!

In the end, we decided to take Trap to the hospital. We figured he probably hadn't had a checkup in a while, and it wouldn't **hurt** him to get one. Well, okay . . . maybe it would **hurt** a little.

The **Old Mouse City Sickly Center** (OMCSC for short) is **enormouse**, with rooms carved out of the side of a mountain. Unfortunately, as we approached the entrance, we could hear mice (rying and complaining.

Trap stopped walking.

"I don't like the sound of this place," he mumbled. "Maybe we should come back **TOMORROW** or the NEXT DAY or never . . ."

"But, Trap, you need a checkup!" Thea scolded him. "It won't be that bad."

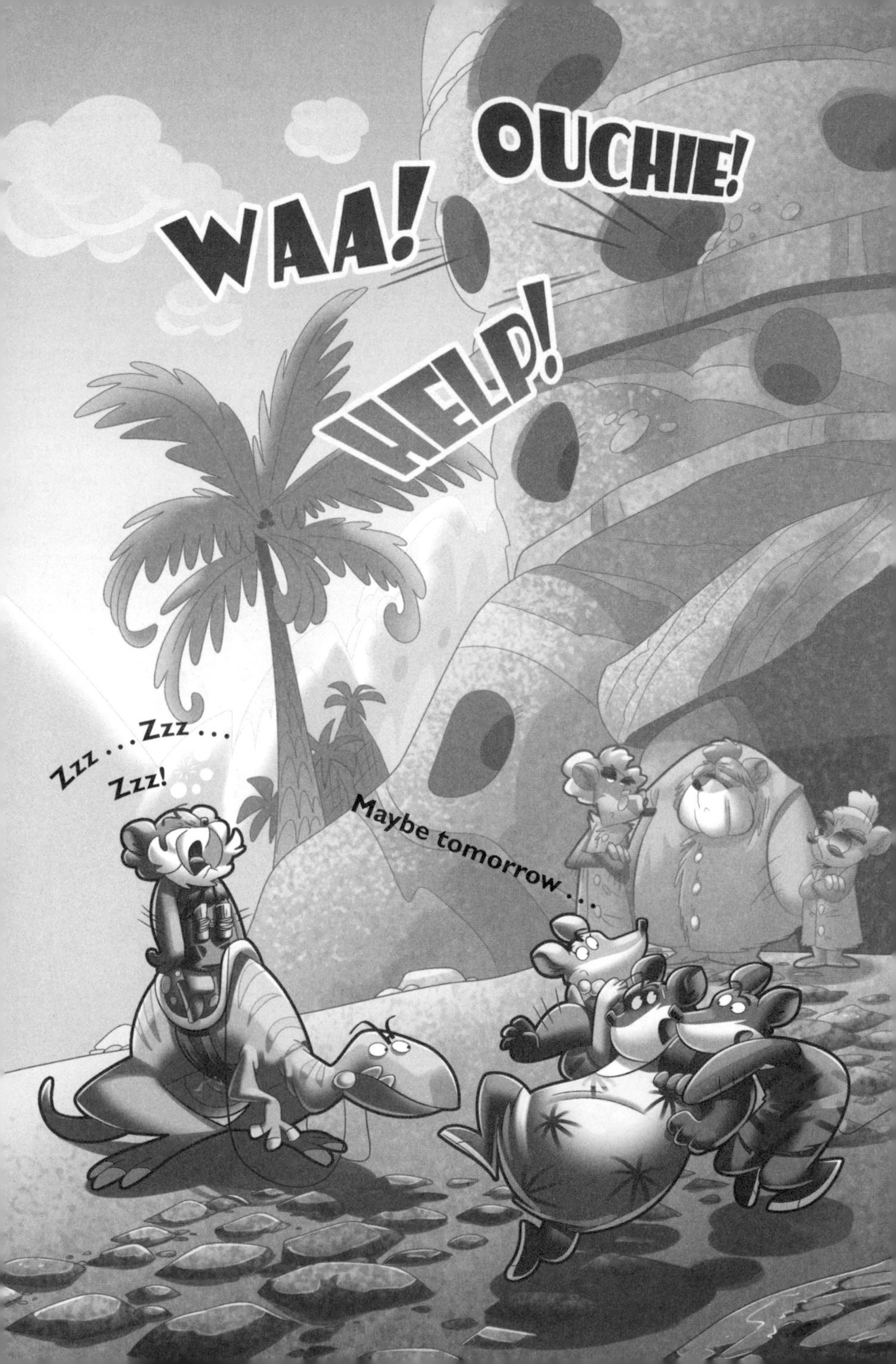
WAA!
OUCHIE!
HELP!
Zzz . . . Zzz . . .
Zzz!
Maybe tomorrow . . .

Finally, we managed to drag him into the hospital, kicking and squeaking.

Even though Pickax was still asleep, he had no problem moving around. He was so used to the STONE AGE SLUMBER he had somehow trained himself to sleepwalk! We watched in amazement as he slid off Grunty and sleepwalked right into the OMCSC!

Before long, I found myself surrounded by a group of three doctors.

"Oh, look who it is!" the first doctor exclaimed. "It's GERONIMO STILTONOOT, the newspaper mouse!"

"You're looking a bit pale, Stiltonoot. Maybe you need a little checkup, too," the second doctor suggested.

"Actually, I feel fine," I replied.

But the doctors didn't listen.

"Stick out your tongue!" the first doctor

So slimy!

!?!

ordered. "It's so SLIMY!"

Next, the second doctor tapped my knee with a hammer. **YOUCH!**

"You're so **sensitive**!" he commented.

Luckily, Thea **dragged** me away before I really got hurt!

"Gotta run!" she called. And she wasn't kidding. At that moment, Trap was racing after the **sleepwalking** Pickax. Suddenly, Pickax woke up.

"What were we **squeaking** about?" he asked as if nothing had happened.

So sensitive!

THUMP!

Youch!

"You said you know someone who can find the **pee-yoo flower**," Thea reminded him.

"Ah, yes!" Pickax replied. "The journalist Sally Rockmousen!"

FOSSiLiZeD Feta! Not my historic (I mean *pre*historic) rival, the head of Gossip Radio, and the most dishonest, fur-pulling cavemouse of the Stone Age!

WHAT A MEGALITHIC MESS!

NURSE! NURSE!

Ask rotten **Sally Rockmousen** for help? I felt **sick** just thinking about it. Still, someone needed to get Trap that antidote, and Sally was our only h⊙pe.

My sister agreed. "Well, we're in the right place," she said. "Last night I heard a nabosaurus* stole Sally's purse. She **hurt** her paw chasing after him, and she's in the hospital."

"Great! Let's go find her!" Pickax suggested.

In fact, Sally was lying on a ROCK BED in the room next door.

* The nabosaurus is a small dinosaur famous for its Jurassic mischief!

Her stomach was **swollen**, and her fur was covered in green spots. How strange! When she saw all of us enter the room, her eyes **WIDENED** in surprise. Then she began to shout.

"What are you doing here? I didn't invite you! **NURSE! NURSE!**"

Pickax put a 🐾🐾🐾 over Sally's mouth before she could make too much noise.

"Shh!" he whispered. "We need your help with something really important!"

"**PALEO PICKAX!**" Sally exclaimed. "Why did you bring these *fools*? Don't you know that **GERONIMO STILTONOOT** is the worst journalist in all of prehistory?"

Pickax explained about Trap, the **snoozer fly**, the STONE AGE SLUMBER, and the antidote from the **putrid pee-yoo** flower.

Sally **ROLLED** her eyes. "Why should I

help?" she screeched. "I would rather get mauled by a deranged SABER-TOOTHED TIGER than HELP Geronimo!"

"Please, Sally," Pickax pleaded. "We only have **THREE DAYS** to find that flower!"

Eventually, Sally agreed, but naturally she wanted something in return.

"You should never do a *favor* for **FREE**, right?" She chuckled.

I was dying to point out to Sally that *favors* should actually *always* be **FREE**, but I figured that would just annoy her. So I chewed my whiskers and kept quiet.

"I want the **exclusive** news story about the discovery of the putrid pee-yoo flower!" Sally demanded. "And most of all: **I want to get out of here and come with you!**"

Thea shook her head. "The doctors will never let you leave," she reasoned. "And by

the way, how did you end up swollen and covered in spots? I thought you hurt your paw while *CHASING* a nabosaurus!"

Sally smirked. "That's the news I spread around. The truth is, I ate a rotten **JURaSSic WaTeRMeLoN**, and, well, I blew up."

"*I'VE GOT IT!*" Pickax announced. He rummaged through his pockets.

Eat it!

First, he pulled out a SMALL SHOVEL, then a BEARD TRIMMER, then a prehistoric **bowling ball**! *How did he fit it all in there?!* Finally, he produced a SMALL RED PEPPER.

"This is a *special* red pepper from the **FIRE LANDS**," he explained. "It's a proven **remedy** that will cure the effects of a rotten Jurassic watermelon!"

He pawed it to Sally.

"Go ahead, Sally!" he said encouragingly. **"Eat it!"**

Sally made a **disgusted** face.

"Sally, it's the only way to cure you and get you out of here," said Pickax.

She took the pepper and ate it.

"Everyone under the bed," Pickax ordered. **"Quickly!"**

Soon we found out why. Sally's eyes shot open, and she began to **bounce** from one wall to the other like a deflating balloon.

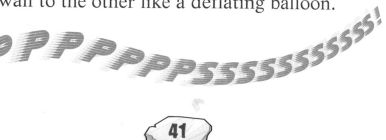

41

As she was deflating, she banged into everything she came in contact with.

In the end, Sally landed on the bed. She returned to her usual size, and the green spots had disappeared completely.

"You should have warned me that would happen, Cheddarface," Sally said.

The doctors were **stunned** by Sally's recovery. They ran tests and scratched their snouts in confusion. They finally gave her permission to leave the hospital.

BUMP

THUMP

CRACK

Too bad Sally hadn't lost her **rotten** personality along with the **green spots**!

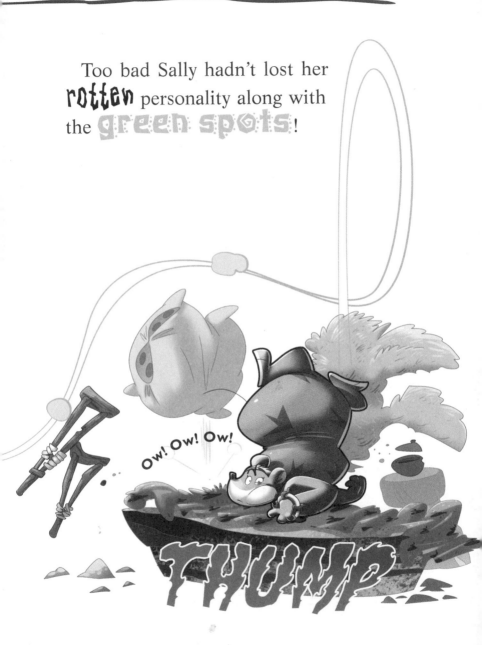

WHAT A PALEOZOIC PRINCESS!

Once we left the hospital, Sally gave us directions.

"First, we need to cross the **desert**," she said.

We began our trek under the **sizzling sun**. As soon as we began, I got the **strangest** feeling that someone was following us. I tried to tell the others, but Thea said I was being a 'fraidy mouse.

Meanwhile, Sally complained nonstop. "This air is too **HOT**! This sand is too **HOT**! This wind is too **HOT**!"

Bones and stones, what a **Paleozoic princess**!

A few minutes later, Sally dug her paws into the sand and declared, "That's it! I'm stopping here!"

"But you can't stop!" wailed Trap. "We only have **THREE DAYS** to find the antidote! It's the only way I can get rid of this STONE AGE SLUMBER! Don't be such a Jurassic whiner!"

"I see only one solution," Sally replied

Faster, faster!

Pant, pant . . .

with a shrug. "Geronimo will have to **CARRY** me the rest of the way!"

Mouse-smashing meteor showers!

Why was Sally such an impossible cavemouse?!

I wanted to tell her to go jump in a hot, **bubbling** volcanic crater, but what could I do? Trap needed my help.

And so, with a heavy sigh, I agreed.

As Thea, Trap, and Pickax continued walking, I barely moved a PAWSTEP. Sally was seated on top of my backpack, and she kept slipping off! When the sun set (*finally!*), I nearly wept TEARS of Jurassic joy. Thank goodmouse for some relief from the HEAT! I was sweating so much I looked just like Leo Edistone's latest invention, the water spitter.

But now that the sun had gone down, the temperature took a drastic NOSEDIVE. Before long, my teeth began chattering. I was f-f-f-freezing!

"Can't you keep still, Geronimo?" Sally complained. "I'm going to fall!"

Eventually, we decided to set up camp for the night.

Thea rubbed some FLINT together to

start a **FIRE**. Then we sat around the flames and warmed up some tasty **Paleolithic cheese**.

Just as I began to **chomp** into my dinner, Sally began to whine.

"This isn't enough cheese for me," she squeaked. "I'm going to need more if you want me to help you."

FOSSILIZED FETA, Sally was such a grumbler!

Sighing, I gave her my portion and slipped into my sleeping bag.

Pickax and Trap immediately fell asleep, but Thea and I were wide-awake. The sound of my stomach **growling** was so loud it kept us both from getting any shut-eye!

Grumble, grumble, growl!

Sally couldn't **sleep**, either.

"I must have eaten too much cheese," she

squeaked. "I know, why don't you two sing me a **lullaby**? You don't have to, of course, but if I don't get enough **sleep**, I won't be able to walk much tomorrow . . ."

Thea and I glared at Sally. But we had no choice. So we began to sing:

"Rockabye, mousey, on the treetop . . ."

Then, in the middle of our serenade, someone **POPPED** up from the desert sand. It was **TIGER KHAN**! Two other saber-toothed tigers from the nasty **BAND OF FELINES** sidled up beside him.

"Tell me the **remedy** for the **STONE AGE SLUMBER**!" Tiger Khan roared at Sally.

Sally began *whistling* nervously. Then she coughed.

"I have no idea what you're talking about," she muttered. "I don't know what kind of *flower* you're talking about."

"Aha!" Tiger Khan shrieked. "You said something about a *flower*! So you **DO** know about the remedy!"

But before the tigers could grab Sally, a strong wind *BLEW* them away.

"Sandstorm!" Pickax yelled.

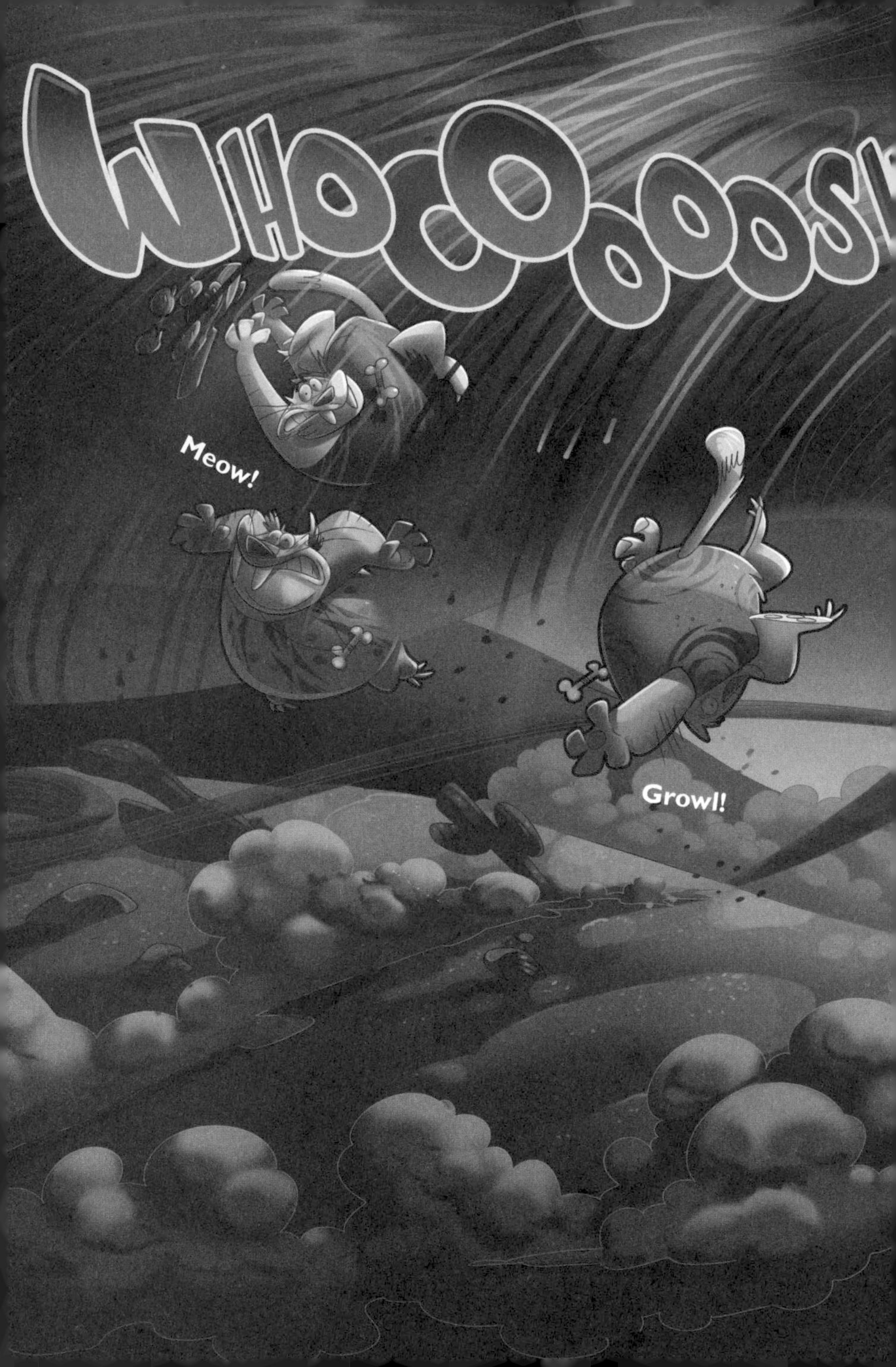
WHOOOOOOS
Meow!
Growl!

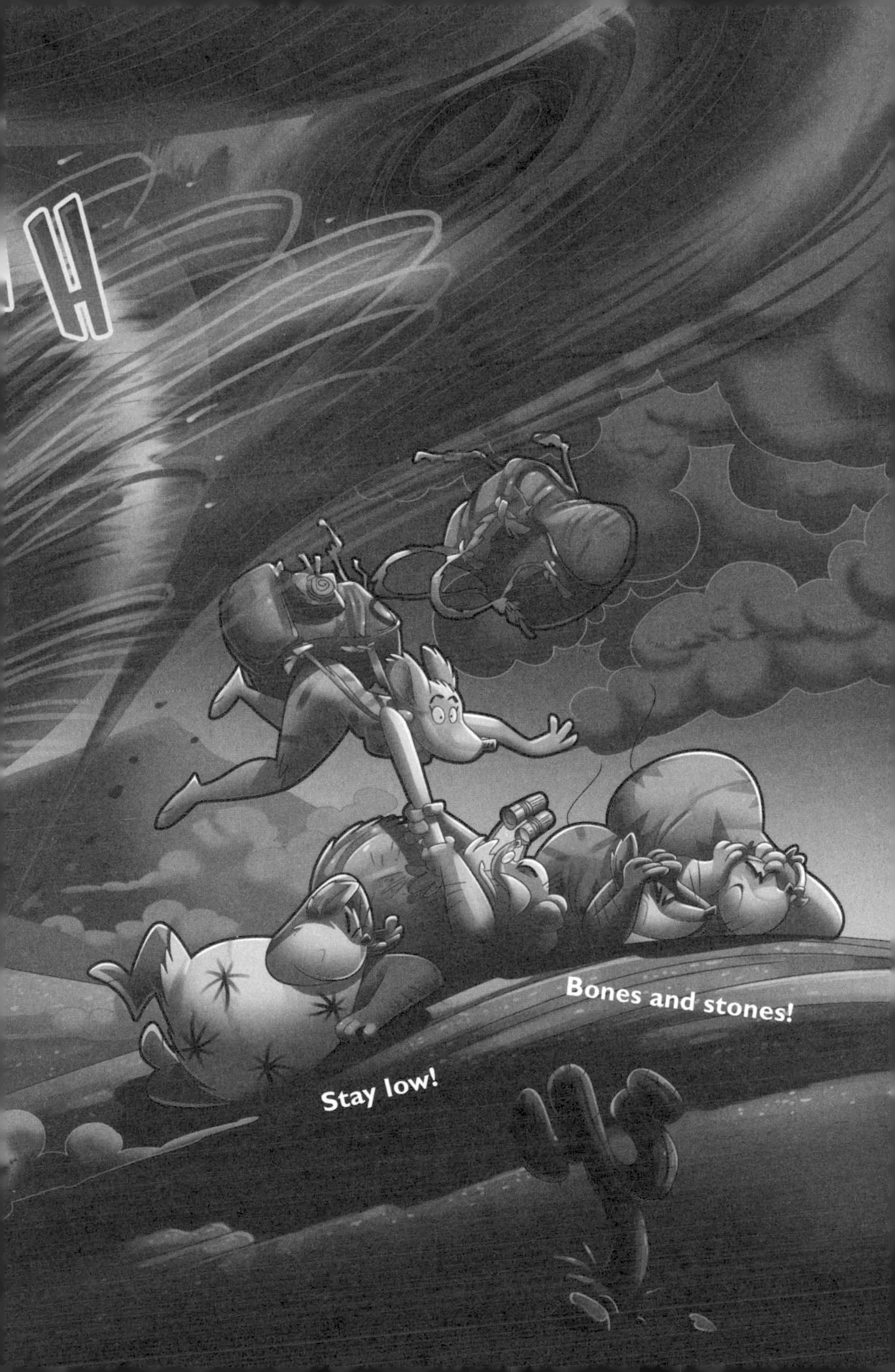
Bones and stones!
Stay low!

WHOOSH!

We slipped into our sleeping bags, but the storm was really **STRONG** and incredibly **scary**!

"Stay **calm**," Pickax reassured us. "It will pass."

"But when will it stop?" I asked, my teeth **chattering**.

"Oh, it should probably be over in —"

FOSSILIZED FETA! As usual, Pickax had fallen asleep at the worst time!

In the end, the storm calmed down, and

we all fell asleep. This time, we slept like PETRIFIED LOGS. We were wiped out!

At DAWN, we woke up. Our whiskers were covered in sand. "Uh-oh!" Trap squeaked. "**Look at that!**"

My heart began to race. Was it **TIGER KHAN**? A **T. REX**? I turned to discover a **GIANT DUNE** blocking our way!

How would I ever be able to climb up that MONSTROUS MOUNTAIN?

Oh no!

"Um, maybe you all should go ahead," I suggested.

"**Forget** it, Gerrykins!" My sister snorted. "We're all going together! Now, **COME ON**!"

And so, huffing and puffing, I began the megalithic climb. **BACK-BREAKING BOULDERS**, it was exhausting!

Eventually, we made it to the top. Then, before we could celebrate, we were hit with another sandstorm!

WHOOSH!

We hid in our sleeping bags. The good news was the storm passed quickly. **The bad news** was it left a new sand mountain bigger than the last one!

PETRIFIED PARMESAN, WHY DO THESE THINGS ALWAYS HAPPEN TO ME?!

"Come on, Stiltonoot, don't be a wet swamp noodle!" Sally spat. "We need to get moving if you want to find that flower!"

I started climbing. I climbed and climbed.

When I arrived at the top, my tongue was hanging from my mouth like a **prehistoric vine**!

"Well, that's it for me," I announced. "I'm going to take a nice little **nap** now."

"What are you **SQUEAKING** about, Geronimo?" Pickax asked. "This is the fun part. We're done with climbing. Now we get

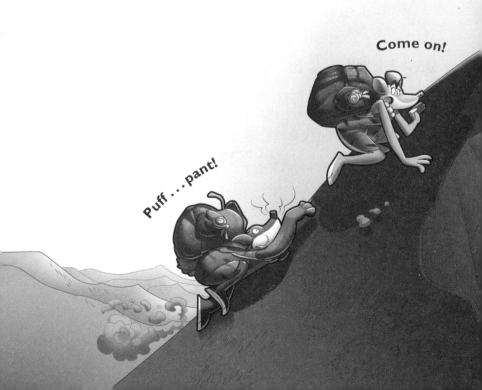

to **roll** down the mountain!"

And with that, he *curled* into a ball and threw himself down the dune.

"**YAHOO!**" he yelled as he **rolled** faster and faster. "Follow me, mice!"

Trap went next, followed by Sally.

Thea stared at me. "Well, what are you 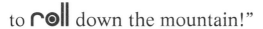 for, Gerrykins?" she asked.

Wahoo!

I gulped, pointing at all the rocks, thorny bushes, and **Paleolithic cacti** below. "I don't want to roll into **that**!" I cried.

"So many **Stone Age excuses**," Thea exclaimed, giving me a shove. "Just go!"

"GOOD-BYE, CAVEMOUSE WORLD!" I wailed as I began to roll.

To my shock, somehow I managed to avoid the sharp stones and pointy branches. I even dodged two cacti, six blackberry bushes, and a super **POISONOUS** desert scorpion!

When I arrived at the bottom, I was all in one piece without a single scratch on me! *Bones and stones, what luck!*

When I looked around, I gasped. In front of me was an oasis. I saw trees, flowers, and a **cool**, **CLEAR** lake.

HOLEY BOULDERS, IT WAS INCREDIBLE!

I jumped into the lake and . . . **WHOMP!**
I ended up with my snout in the sand!
That was no **oasis** — it was a **mirage**!

IT'S JUST A MIRAGE!

Now, I don't know if you know (and if you don't know, I'll tell you), but in the desert, it's easy to find mirages. The HOT air, the SCORCHING sand, and the BURNING sun can create optical illusions that make a mouse see things like WATER when there's really only sand!

After my lake mistake, I began walking again. Then it happened a **second** time! A lavish feast fit for royalty appeared before me. I saw **tasty** cheeses, **cold** drinks, and **juicy**, colorful fruits. I threw myself at the table of treats. Instantly, the table disappeared. **Rats!**

Sally **SNORTED** with laughter.

"Ha, ha, ha!" she cackled. "Stiltonoot, you're a **MESS**!"

I ignored her. Only the **rotten** Sally Rockmousen would **KICK** a mouse when hc's already down!

As I trudged along, I continued to see mirages. First, I saw a pot of **volcanic fondue**.

Next, I saw a **MAMMOTH MILKSHAKE**. I did my best to resist the urge to taste

each treat. Oh, how I hated mirages!

We climbed up a tall dune and down the other side. At the bottom, I spotted another oasis complete with a lake and lots of green vegetation.

Oh no, I'm not falling for this again, I told myself. *It's just a mirage.*

But right then I spotted something — or rather, some*one* — I couldn't resist. I spied Clarissa Conjurat, the shaman Bluster's daughter, leaning against a palm tree! It was really her, the

Clarissa, my sweet!

rodent of my *dreams*! She greeted me with a friendly smile and waved her paw.

"Clarissa, is it really you?!" I squeaked. I couldn't believe my luck. What are the chances my **secret crush** would find me in the desert?

I ran toward her, paws outstretched until . . .

BONK!

I ended up smacking right into a Jurassic palm tree!

BONES AND STONES, IT WAS YET ANOTHER MIRAGE!

When I looked up, I saw that Trap, Thea, Pickax, and Sally had reached an oasis. I saw PARROTS, TOUCANS, and other multicolored birds perched in swaying palm trees. I saw a **woolly mammoth** and a pterodactyl happily drinking from a crystal lake. Could it be?

As I looked closer, I saw Thea and Pickax SPLASHING themselves with water as Sally dipped her paws at one end of the pool. It all looked amazingly real, but I was no fool. I wasn't going to get tricked again.

"Come on, Cuz," Trap said, jumping into the lake. "What are you waiting for?"

Not again, I told myself, closing my eyes.

For the love of **cheese**, these mirages could drive a mouse crazy!

At that moment, the most **FABUMOUSE** surprise happened. I was hit by a shower of **cold** water! My eyes flew open. **SWEET, SUN-WARMED SWISS!** A woolly mammoth had just doused me with lake water!

This place was **real** after all!

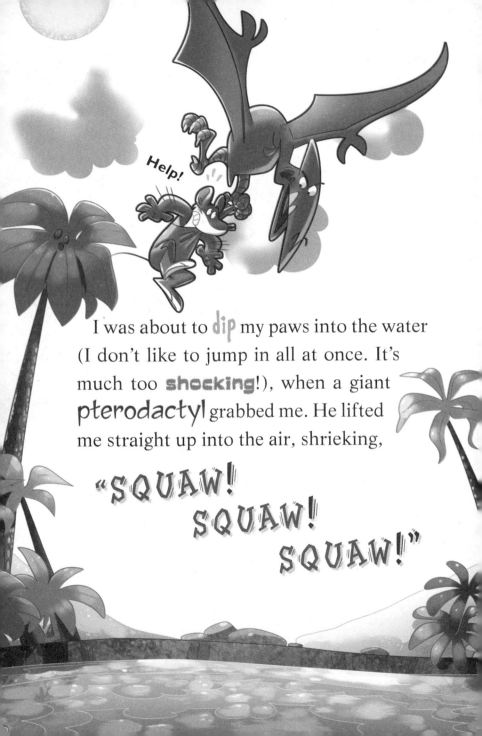

Help!

I was about to **dip** my paws into the water
(I don't like to jump in all at once. It's
much too **shocking**!), when a giant
pterodactyl grabbed me. He lifted
me straight up into the air, shrieking,

"SQUAW!
  SQUAW!
     SQUAW!"

"Bones and stones, I'm afraid of heights!" But the bird kept on soaring higher and higher.

Then, with one final SQUAW!, he dropped me into the center of the lake!

SPLASH!

Holey boulders, what a mouserific plunge!

The mammoth stuck his trunk in the water and began blowing **bubbles**. He was creating the first **hot tub** of the Stone Age! Have you ever been in one? Let me tell you, it was super relaxing. For a while, I even felt like all my troubles were floating away . . .

Of course, it wasn't long before I had to return to reality.

"So where is this pee-yoo flower?" Thea asked Sally, searching some nearby shrubs.

"The flower isn't here," Sally explained, pointing to a **HUGE** hill. "It's on top of that mountain."

Rats! Not another climb!

Since it was almost evening, Pickax proposed that we begin the climb at dawn.

"But tomorrow is the end of the **THREE** days!" Thea objected.

Pickax nodded, but insisted that climbing in the dark would be too dangerous. In the end, we all agreed and set up camp.

The mammoth (whose name was **WOOLBUR**) and the pterodactyl (who we named Squaw) joined us. The bird rested in a palm tree while the rest of us curled up around Woolbur.

Right before I fell asleep, I thought I saw

two shapes hiding in the shadows . . .

WAS IT THE SABER-TOOTHED TIGERS AGAIN?!

I couldn't say. I was too tired to find out. Within minutes, I was snoring away like a cavesaw.

ZZZZZZZ!

ROOOARRR!

The next morning, Pickax got everything we needed for the climb, including braided vines, spikes, and granite hooks.

"I'll take a rain check on the exhausting climb," Sally announced.

So we left her behind and started climbing.

HOLEY BOULDERS, IT WAS EXHAUSTING!

I was congratulating myself on my progress when suddenly I SLIPPED. The next thing I knew, I was dangling like a Mesozoic madmouse from the edge of a STEEP CLIFF!

"Help!" I yelled, my whiskers trembling.

Luckily, Thea managed to grab the end of the vine I had **wrapped** around me. Trap and Pickax rushed over. Together, the three of them pulled me up the **ROCKY** cliff.

Phew . . . saved by a whisker! My heart was still hammering like a prehistoric woodpecker when we entered the **big cloud** that hid the top of the mountain. Immediately, a **FREEZING RAIN** soaked our fur.

"Let's take **shelter** in there!" Thea yelled, pointing to a cave on the side of the mountain.

Gulp!

It was so **DARK** in the cave we couldn't see much, but we were too **exhausted** to care.

"I'm so tired, I could sleep for a week!" Trap yawned.

"I'm so tired, even this **ROUGH ROCK** seems comfortable!" Thea added.

"**ROUGH ROCK?**" I exclaimed. "I guess I got lucky because I found a really **soft** blanket."

I was about to drift off to sleep when suddenly . . .

RRRROOOAAAARRRRR!

A megalithic growl filled the cave.

BONES AND STONES! That was no blanket! It was a wild, **FEROCIOUS** cave bear!

Terrified, I closed my eyes. Was I about to become just another grizzly STONE AGE STATISTIC?

But at that moment, the stra̋ngest thing happened. Pickax approached the bear, looked it in the eye, and . . . burst out laughing!

"Hey, you're not a **scary** cave bear!" Pickax exclaimed. "You're my old friend **BEARBIE**!" Pickax said.

The bear greeted Pickax with a big **BEAR HUG**. Then Pickax explained that during one

PICKAX APPROACHED THE BEAR . . .

of his legendary explorations, he had saved Bearbie from the grips of an iceosaurus (a polar T. rex). Apparently, Bearbie used to live in the POLAR LANDS before she decided she preferred a milder climate.

Bearbie offered us some prehistoric MOUNTAIN HONEY. It was delicious! A moment later, Pickax and Trap fell into their STONE AGE SLUMBER.

LOOKED IT IN THE EYES . . .

AND THE TWO OF THEM HUGGED!

"Come on, Ger! Let's go get those **pee-yoo petals**!" my sister suggested.

I wasn't thrilled about climbing more cliffs, but I couldn't say no to Thea. And we were on a **DEADLINE**! So with Bearbie watching over our sleeping friends, we set off. Thanks to my sister, one of the most **ATHLETIC** rodents in prehistory, we climbed to the top without any trouble. (Well, okay, I was **huffing** and **puffing**, but that's between you and me.)

When we arrived at the peak, we finally saw them — the infamouse pee-yoo flowers! At first glance, they didn't look like much,

though they were a strange shade of GREEN. But then we got a *whiff* of them.

PEE-YOO! Those flowers stunk more than my cousin Trap when he hasn't bathed for an entire geological era!

"Ugh, what a stench!" I moaned.

"Reminds me of a stinky mouse!" a voice called out.

Holey boulders!

It was TIGER KHAN!

CREAK! CRICK! CRACK!

I couldn't believe it! **TIGER KHAN** and his henchcats had beaten us to the flowers! They weren't troubled at all by the stench. (After all, they're accustomed to the stink of **Bugville**, the swamp where they live.) The tigers had already gathered a bunch of **flowers** in their claws.

FOSSILIZED FETA! What terrible luck we were having!

It turns out those rotten saber-toothed tigers had been following us for **miles** and **miles** and **miles**!

"How dare you spy on us!" Thea shrieked. The tigers roared with laughter.

"If it weren't for that **flea-ridden mammoth** protecting you, we would have already turned you into **mouse kebabs**!" one of the giant cats snarled.

Just then I realized we had left Woolbur behind. **GULP!** Who would come to our rescue now?

"Get them!" Tiger Khan shouted as he reached for me with his claws.

I covered my eyes. My heart *RACED* and my whiskers *shook*. Great **RUMBLING** lava explosions! I was having a prehistoric panic attack!

But then nothing happened. I opened my eyes and . . .

ZZZZZZzzzZzZzzZZZzzZzzzZzzz!

Tiger Khan was sleeping as soundly as a kitten! Phew! The STONE AGE SLUMBER

had knocked him out just in time!

Even though Tiger Khan was sleeping, the other saber-toothed tigers were very much awake. Thea and I began to run at LIGHTNING SPEED along the edge of the TREACHEROUS cliffs.

"Give up, you little cave vermin!" the saber-toothed tigers roared at us. "Sooner or later, we're going to win!"

Unfortunately, SOONER came a lot faster than LATER. I was doing my best trying to keep up with Thea when I got a little too close to the edge.

"Careful, Ger!" Thea shouted.

But it was too late. I lost my balance and fell into the abyss, tumbling down the mountain.

"I DON'T WANT TO BE EXTINCT!" I yelled, my cry echoing off the rocks.

The good news was that
I managed to grab on to a
shrub that was **poking** out
of the rocks. The bad news
was that the plant was too
fragile, and the roots
began to slowly give
way.

CREEEAK!
CRIIICK!
CRAAACK!

I could already picture
myself spread flat like **cream**
cheese in the sun when
a sharp sound broke the
silence of the mountain . . .

SQUAW!
SQUAW!
SQUAW!

Whoops!

Oh no!

Help!

A shadow fell over me as a *flying* dinosaur came into view. It was Squaw, our pterodactyl friend. With nimble claws, he grabbed me by the paw and lifted me **UP** into the air.

"Thanks, Squaw!" I squeaked, breathing a sigh of relief. But there was no time to celebrate. My sister was fighting off **vicious** Tiger Khan and his henchcats, and she was all alone!

We rushed to Bearbie's cave, where I quickly explained the situation. Then the bear, the bird, and I hurried back to the top of the mountain, leaving Trap and Pickax still **SLUMBERING** away.

Bearbie was an agile climber, and she had no problem scaling the **JAGGED** mountain cliffs. I was so exhausted I had to hitch a ride with the **GIANT** pterodactyl!

Once we got to the top, we spotted Thea **hurling** sharp rocks at the saber-toothed tigers. In fact, many of the nasty cats were already sprouting **MEGALITHIC-SIZED** bumps on their heads!

The saber-toothed beasts were super angry, but before they could fight back, Bearbie reached the top of the mountain.

ROOOOAAAAARRR!

"A bear!" cried the cats. "Run for your lives!"

Bearbie raced after the pack, but the saber-toothed tigers were quicker than a bunch of velociraptors. They grabbed the sleeping Tiger Khan and took off, meowing like frightened kittens.

"S-s-sorry, M-M-Mister Bear," stammered one saber-toothed tiger.

"We w-w-won't b-b-bother you again," added another.

Bearbie let out a loud **ROAR** in response, which sent the frightened felines rolling down the mountain like sacks of **Paleozoic potatoes**.

"The bear isn't a mister!" Thea yelled after them. "She's a miss!"

Once the tigers had disappeared, we thanked Bearbie for her help. Then we quickly got busy gathering the **pee-yoo flowers**.

Yuck! I'd make a bet their stench was the most disgusting smell in all prehistory! I held my nose as I **PLUCKED** the flowers. What else could I do? Trap's health was in my paws!

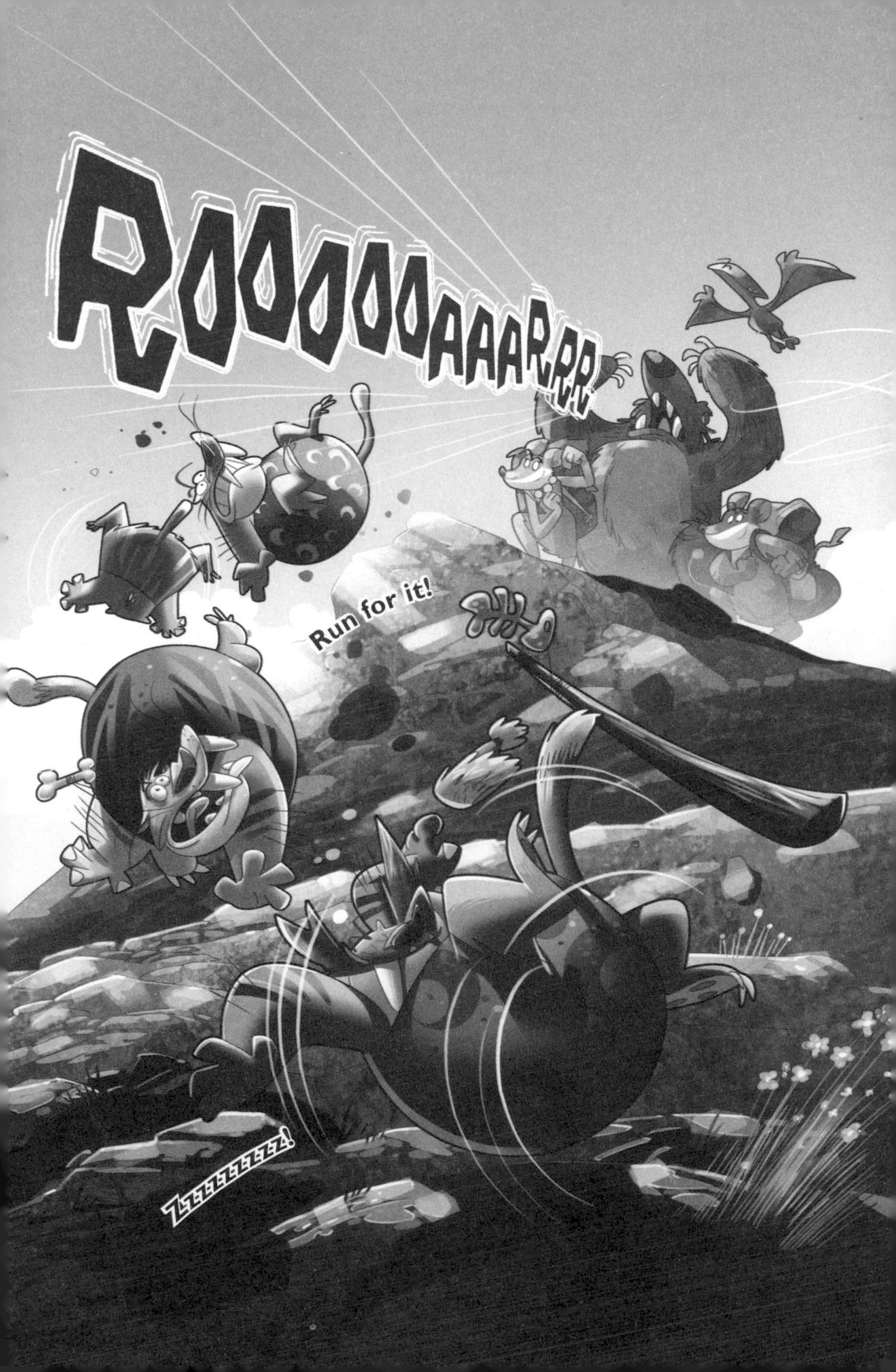
ROOOOOAAARRR
Run for it!
ZZZZZZZZZZ!

When we all returned to Bearbie's den, Trap and Pickax had just woken up from their STONE AGE SLUMBER.

"Okay!" my cousin exclaimed, JUMPING to his feet. "Let's get moving! Why is everyone standing around? Let's go find those flowers!"

"Yes! Yes!" Pickax agreed. "Time is running out!"

No one moved a whisker. Instead, we started laughing. Trap and Pickax scratched their heads in confusion until Thea explained what had happened. She held up the bunch of freshly picked pee-yoo flowers, waving them in the air like a TROPHY.

"Aw, thanks, cousins!" Trap squeaked. "I knew I could count on you!"

Pickax broke up our lovefest with a dose of

REALITY. "Our **MISSION** isn't over yet! We need to make that tea! The **THREE DAYS** are almost up!" he reminded us.

Thanks, cousins!

PEE-YOO TEA

We scampered down to the foot of the mountain as fast as we could go without **BREAKING** our tails! I'm too fond of my tail!

When we arrived, we found the band of saber-toothed tigers surrounding a sleeping **TIGER KHAN**. Yep, he was still under the **STONE AGE SLUMBER**! Lucky for us, the cats were having no luck trying to wake their boss.

We also found my nemesis, Sally Rockmousen, busily preparing a huge pot of boiling water for the tea. **Holey cheese chunks!** Had Sally turned over a new cave leaf? Was she really being helpful?

I wanted to ask, but time was running out. We had to get the tea brewing. We began pulling the petals off the pee-yoo flowers and tossing them into the **bubbling** cauldron. It didn't take long before a terrible stench **ROSE** from the boiling water.

Snort!

Bones and stones, it stunk! The **SMELL** was so strong that the toucans, parrots, and hummingbirds stopped *singing* and flew away, disgusted. Even Woolbur tied a knot in his trunk to keep out the **foul odor**!

Finally, the tea was ready. Pickax poured it into a bowl and told Trap to drink it.

"Ugh," my cousin protested, wrinkling his nose. "I can't drink this slop! The **stench** is worse than the breath of a **SKUNK WEED**–eating T. rex!"

Pickax **snorted**. "If you prefer not to smell the **STINK**,

I can club you over the head," he offered.

After all the trouble we had gone to finding the remedy, it was pretty clear no one was moving a whisker until Trap drank that tea!

Reluctantly, Trap lifted the bowl to his snout and **GULPED** down the whole thing.

"Mmm . . . you know, it's not so bad," he admitted, smacking his lips when he was done. "It reminds me a bit of the curdled milk used in mammoth milkshakes . . . ahh, the taste of home!"

Then he peeked into the pot. "I just might DRINK the rest of it!" he declared.

But at that moment, we noticed the pack of tigers looking at their leader sadly. Yes, Tiger Khan is a **FEROCIOUS**, nasty cat who's always trying to make **mice meat** out of us for dinner. But a real cavemouse always

PUTRID PEE-YOO TEA

INGREDIENTS FOR ONE SERVING (IT'S RARE TO FIND MORE THAN ONE CAVEMOUSE AT A TIME WHO WANTS TO TRY IT!):

- A BUNCH OF PEE-YOO FLOWER PETALS
- A CLOVE OF GARLIC
- SUGAR TO TASTE
- COURAGE!

INSTRUCTIONS: PUT THE PETALS INTO A POT OF BOILING WATER UNTIL THEY BEGIN TO DISINTEGRATE. THEN OPEN THE WINDOWS AND RUN OUT OF THE KITCHEN BECAUSE THE STENCH WILL BE HORRIBLE!

AFTER A FEW MINUTES, TAKE THE POT OFF THE FIRE AND POUR THE INFUSION INTO A BOWL. USE A CLOTHESPIN TO PLUG YOUR NOSE, THEN TAKE A SIP OF THE STINKIEST TEA IN ALL OF PREHISTORY!

SIDE EFFECTS: FOR A FEW HOURS AFTERWARD, NO CAVEMICE WILL WANT TO BE ANYWHERE NEAR YOU!

helps others and doesn't hold a grudge.

So we carved out a little funnel from a Jurassic **palm leaf** and made the leader of the band of felines drink the infusion while he was still **asleep**.

The saber-toothed tigers looked at us without a word, until . . .

BOING!!!

Tiger Khan opened his eyes and **POPPED** up like a spring. **TEARS** sprang to his eyes as he stared fondly at his henchcats standing over him.

"So you aren't the **good-for-nothings** I thought you were!" he exclaimed, hugging each one. "You made me the tea!"

The saber-toothed tigers guiltily confessed that, in fact, we cavemice had actually

prepared and **shared** the tea.

Tiger Khan was livid. He looked like he was about to **EXPLODE** into a thousand **furry** pieces. "You fools! How could you let a bunch of **CAVEMICE** save me?! Don't you realize I have a reputation to uphold? My *prestige* as a FEROCIOUS cavemouse eater? My *fame* as a **ruthless** saber-toothed tiger? My **status** as the great leader of the band of felines?"

Tiger Khan marched off, still ranting and lashing his tail back and forth in disgust. "What a bunch of kittens!" he roared. "Can't you cats get anything right?"

The pack followed behind him, heads hung low. Trying to explain what happened to their leader without getting him riled up was like trying to fly. It was IMPOSSIBLE!

Soon the humiliated cats disappeared over the horizon. At last we were rid of those PALEOZOIC pests!

Just then I noticed Pickax staring wistfully at the few drops of tea left in the pot. Even though years had passed, I encouraged him to try some. Hey, you never know. Maybe he could cure his own STONE AGE SLUMBER.

So Pickax took a bowl and filled it with the stinky concoction. Then he drank it

down quickly as we watched, holding our breath.

GLUG GLUG GLUG GLUG . . .

When he was finished, he wiped his mouth with the back of his paw and smiled. "Ahhh, I feel so **young** again!" he squeaked. "So full of energy! So *alive*!"

"Really?" Trap asked skeptically. "You feel awake?"

"Awake?!" Pickax repeated. "I've never felt more awake in my life! I'm more awake than I've been in —"

ZZZZZZZZZZZ!

Before he could finish his sentence, he

fell into his STONE AGE SLUMBER!

Bones and stones, too much time had passed since the **snoozer fly** had stung him! It was **TOO LATE** for the tea remedy. Thea, Trap, and I looked at one another. At first we felt bad that Pickax couldn't be cured. But in the end we decided he was PERFECT the way he was!

Glug, glug, glug!

Wow!

ZZZZZZ

SPREAD THE WORD!

As soon as we reached Old Mouse City, the staff of Radio Gossip ran to meet us.

"I have the most amazing news! Get ready to spread it!" Sally shouted, clearing her throat dramatically. "The most beautiful, courageous, intelligent, charming, compassionate, modest, and humble Sally Rockmousen has heroically come to the aid of Trap Stiltonoot and cured him of the STONE AGE SLUMBER!"

When Sally's staff didn't repeat the message immediately, she shrieked. "Well, what are you waiting for, fools? SPREAD THE WORD!"

The first crier climbed to the top of a tall ladder, took a giant breath, and threw back his head. Then he yelled:

"Sally Rockmousen saves Trap Stiltonoot from the Stone Age Slumber!"

The second crier gargled with salt water, smoothed her whiskers, patted her large stomach, and shrieked:

"SALLY ROCKMOUSEN SHAVES TRAP STILTONOOT AND STONE AGE PLUMBER!"

The third crier performed some deep-breathing exercises, then called out:

"SALLY ROCKMOUSEN CRAVES TRAP STILTONOOT THE STONE AGE DRUMMER!"

We couldn't help giggling over Gossip Radio's ridiculous broadcast. As usual, they made a mammoth **mess** of the story.

Sally Rockmousen saves Trap Stiltonoot from the Stone Age Slumber!
Sally Rockmousen shaves Trap Stiltonoot and Stone Age plumber!
Grrrr!

Meanwhile, Sally **clenched** her teeth in rage.

Eventually, the citizens of Old Mouse City got the real **scoop** and began congratulating Sally and asking for her *autograph*.

"Oh, it was nothing," Sally told her small crowd of admirers. "Of course, I had to do EVERYTHING myself, but then again what do you expect from the Stiltonoots?!"

Holey boulders, the old Sally Rockmousen had returned!

But while she was busy bragging, Sally accidentally tripped and fell into a stand of watermelons.

CRASH!

For a second, Sally lay buried underneath the watermelons. She emerged with a **scowl**.

"You sure love **WATERMELONS**!" Trap remarked. "Maybe you shouldn't eat them all, though. Remember the **HOSPITAL**?"

"How dare you!" Sally shrieked, turning as **red** as a Jurassic pepper. "From this moment on, we are going **BACK** to the way things were, my dear Stiltonoots!"

"What do you mean?!" Thea asked, acting surprised. "You mean that a **kind**, modest rodent like you doesn't want to be BFFs with

Humph!

the entire Stiltonoot clan?"

SALLY ROCKMOUSEN glared at all of us, then turned and headed toward the offices of **Gossip Radio**.

I was about to return to my office when Trap stopped me.

"**Hold on**, Cousin!" he squeaked. "Everyone's invited to the **Rotten Tooth Tavern** to celebrate my recovery!"

Right at that moment, Pickax woke up with a snort. He shook his head, got to his feet, and announced, "I think I'll organize an expedition to the **Land of the Sweltering Muggy Weather**. Who's with me?"

A picture of the last three days flashed before my eyes. The **boiling** desert, the **DANGEROUS** cliffs, the mirages, the **TERRIFYING** saber-toothed tigers . . .

"Not me!" I yelled, running toward the

tavern. I had had my share of adventure for the month . . . and possibly for the next two or three **GEOLOGICAL AGES**! That's the truth, or my name isn't

Geronimo Stiltonoot, cavemouse!

Don't miss any adventures of the cavemice!

#1 The Stone of Fire

#2 Watch Your Tail!

#3 Help, I'm in Hot Lava!

#4 The Fast and the Frozen

#5 The Great Mouse Race

#6 Don't Wake the Dinosaur!

#7 I'm a Scaredy-Mouse!

#8 Surfing for Secrets

#9 Get the Scoop, Geronimo!

#10 My Autosaurus Will Win!

Up Next!

#11 Sea Monster Surprise

#12 Paws Off the Pearl!

#13 The Smelly Search

#14 Shoo, Caveflies!

#15 A Mammoth Mystery

Be sure to read all my fabumouse adventures!

#1 Lost Treasure of the Emerald Eye

#2 The Curse of the Cheese Pyramid

#3 Cat and Mouse in a Haunted House

#4 I'm Too Fond of My Fur!

#5 Four Mice Deep in the Jungle

#6 Paws Off, Cheddarface!

#7 Red Pizzas for a Blue Count

#8 Attack of the Bandit Cats

#9 A Fabumouse Vacation for Geronimo

#10 All Because of a Cup of Coffee

#11 It's Halloween, You 'Fraidy Mouse!

#12 Merry Christmas, Geronimo!

#13 The Phantom of the Subway

#14 The Temple of the Ruby of Fire

#15 The Mona Mousa Code

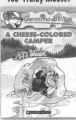

#16 A Cheese-Colored Camper

#17 Watch Your Whiskers, Stilton!

#18 Shipwreck on the Pirate Islands

#19 My Name Is Stilton, Geronimo Stilton

#20 Surf's Up, Geronimo!

#21 The Wild, Wild West

#22 The Secret of Cacklefur Castle

A Christmas Tale

#23 Valentine's Day Disaster

#24 Field Trip to Niagara Falls

#25 The Search for Sunken Treasure

#26 The Mummy with No Name

#27 The Christmas Toy Factory

#28 Wedding Crasher

#29 Down and Out Down Under

#30 The Mouse Island Marathon

#31 The Mysterious Cheese Thief

Christmas Catastrophe

#32 Valley of the Giant Skeletons

#33 Geronimo and the Gold Medal Mystery

#34 Geronimo Stilton, Secret Agent

#35 A Very Merry Christmas

#36 Geronimo's Valentine

#37 The Race Across America

#38 A Fabumouse School Adventure

#39 Singing Sensation

#40 The Karate Mouse

#41 Mighty Mount Kilimanjaro

#42 The Peculiar Pumpkin Thief

#43 I'm Not a Supermouse!

#44 The Giant Diamond Robbery

#45 Save the White Whale!

#46 The Haunted Castle

#47 Run for the Hills, Geronimo!

#48 The Mystery in Venice

#49 The Way of the Samurai

#50 This Hotel Is Haunted!

#51 The Enormouse Pearl Heist

#52 Mouse in Space!

#53 Rumble in the Jungle

#54 Get into Gear, Stilton!

#55 The Golden Statue Plot

#56 Flight of the Red Bandit

The Hunt for the Golden Book

#57 The Stinky Cheese Vacation

#58 The Super Chef Contest

#59 Welcome to Moldy Manor

The Hunt for the Curious Cheese

#60 The Treasure of Easter Island

#61 Mouse House Hunter

#62 Mouse Overboard!

The Hunt for the Secret Papyrus

#63 The Cheese Experiment

#64 Magical Mission

#65 Bollywood Burglary

The Hunt for the Hundredth Key

#66 Operation: Secret Recipe

#67 The Chocolate Chase

Join me and my friends as we travel through time in these very special editions!

THE JOURNEY THROUGH TIME

BACK IN TIME:
THE SECOND JOURNEY THROUGH TIME

THE RACE AGAINST TIME:
THE THIRD JOURNEY THROUGH TIME

LOST IN TIME:
THE FOURTH JOURNEY THROUGH TIME

MEET
Geronimo Stiltonord

He is a mouseking — the Geronimo Stilton of the ancient far north! He lives with his brawny and brave clan in the village of Mouseborg. From sailing frozen waters to facing fiery dragons, every day is an adventure for the micekings!

#1 Attack of the Dragons

#2 The Famouse Fjord Race

#3 Pull the Dragon's Tooth!

#4 Stay Strong, Geronimo!

#5 The Mysterious Message

#6 The Helmet Holdup

Don't miss any of my adventures in the Kingdom of Fantasy!

THE KINGDOM OF FANTASY

THE QUEST FOR PARADISE:
THE RETURN TO THE KINGDOM OF FANTASY

THE AMAZING VOYAGE:
THE THIRD ADVENTURE IN THE KINGDOM OF FANTASY

THE DRAGON PROPHECY:
THE FOURTH ADVENTURE IN THE KINGDOM OF FANTASY

THE VOLCANO OF FIRE:
THE FIFTH ADVENTURE IN THE KINGDOM OF FANTASY

THE SEARCH FOR TREASURE:
THE SIXTH ADVENTURE IN THE KINGDOM OF FANTASY

THE ENCHANTED CHARMS:
THE SEVENTH ADVENTURE IN THE KINGDOM OF FANTASY

THE PHOENIX OF DESTINY:
AN EPIC KINGDOM OF FANTASY ADVENTURE

THE HOUR OF MAGIC:
THE EIGHTH ADVENTURE IN THE KINGDOM OF FANTASY

THE WIZARD'S WAND:
THE NINTH ADVENTURE IN THE KINGDOM OF FANTASY

THE SHIP OF SECRETS:
THE TENTH ADVENTURE IN THE KINGDOM OF FANTASY

THE DRAGON OF FORTUNE:
AN EPIC KINGDOM OF FANTASY ADVENTURE

MEET
GERONIMO STILTONIX

He is a spacemouse — the Geronimo
Stilton of a parallel universe! He is
captain of the spaceship *MouseStar 1*.
While flying through the cosmos, he visits
distant planets and meets crazy aliens.
His adventures are out of this world!

#1 Alien Escape

#2 You're Mine, Captain!

#3 Ice Planet Adventure

#4 The Galactic Goal

#5 Rescue Rebellion

#6 The Underwater
Planet

#7 Beware! Space Junk!

#8 Away in a Star Sled

#9 Slurp Monster
Showdown

#10 Pirate Spacerat
Attack

#11 We'll Bite Your
Tail, Geronimo!

Old Mouse City
(MOUSE ISLAND)

THE CAVE OF MEMORIES

GOSSIP RADIO

THE STONE GAZETTE

TRAP'S HOUSE

THE ROTTEN TOOTH TAVERN

LIBERTY ROCK

UGH UGH CABIN

DINO RIVER

DEAR MOUSE FRIENDS,
THANKS FOR READING,
AND GOOD-BYE UNTIL
THE NEXT BOOK!